The Christmas Unicorn

For Zoë, with love.

OXFORD
UNIVERSITY PRESS

Great Clarendon Street, Oxford OX2 6DP

Oxford University Press is a department of the University of Oxford.
It furthers the University's objective of excellence in research, scholarship,
and education by publishing worldwide in

Oxford New York

Auckland Cape Town Dar es Salaam Hong Kong Karachi
Kuala Lumpur Madrid Melbourne Mexico City Nairobi
New Delhi Shanghai Taipei Toronto

With offices in

Argentina Austria Brazil Chile Czech Republic France Greece
Guatemala Hungary Italy Japan Poland Portugal Singapore
South Korea Switzerland Thailand Turkey Ukraine Vietnam

Oxford is a registered trade mark of Oxford University Press in the UK
and certain other countries

First published 2006
Reissued in 2012

British Library Cataloguing in Publication Data available

ISBN: 978-0-19-279309-6

2 4 6 8 10 9 7 5 3 1

Printed in China

Paper used in the production of this book is a natural, recyclable
product made from wood grown in sustainable forests. The manufacturing
process conforms to the environmental regulations of the country of origin.

The Christmas Unicorn

ANNA CURREY

OXFORD

UNIVERSITY PRESS

'There now, Milly,' said Mum, tucking her in and giving her a good-night kiss. 'Don't look so gloomy. Poor Grandpa would be lonely at Christmas if we didn't come to stay, and Dad will be here just as soon as he can. So good-night, sleep tight!'

But Milly didn't sleep tight.
She knelt at the end of her bed and
gazed over the moonlit snowy fields
to the forest beyond.

From the shadow of the trees an owl, a fox, and a unicorn
looked out. The little town that usually twinkled away
quietly at night was now ablaze with pink, purple, red,
yellow, and blue lights. They flashed and danced
and sparkled.

'What are those lights for?' asked the unicorn.
'For Christmas,' said the fox, who
knew everything.

'Christmas?' wondered the unicorn softly.
'*Christmas!*' he repeated, tossing his
head and kicking his heels.
'I'm going off to see!'
And away he went.

He trotted down the silent
sleeping street, past garden
gates all tightly shut . . .
except for one. He nosed
it open and went in.

The gate made a loud CREAK! Milly opened
her window. She stared at the unicorn
for a very long time. 'Hello,' said Milly.
'Hello,' said the unicorn. And they stared again.
'Wait there!' said Milly suddenly. 'Don't go.'

Milly ran downstairs to open the door and in came the unicorn, along with a few soft flakes of snow.

He pattered across the hall floor and shook himself hard.

'My name's Milly,' whispered Milly. 'What's yours?' 'Florian,' said the unicorn.

'I'm staying at Grandpa's house,' said Milly, stroking Florian's soft silky tail. 'But I wish I had a friend to play with in the snow and I wish Dad was here, too. Mum says he's going to come just as soon as he can.'

Florian said nothing, he had fallen fast asleep. But Milly stayed awake for a long time. 'I've got a unicorn,' she said to herself, 'a unicorn of my very own.'

'I've got a unicorn!' Milly announced the next morning.
'Have you?' said Mum. 'That's nice.'
'Would he like some breakfast?' asked Grandpa
politely, offering Florian a slice of toast.
Florian liked toast. And jam. And muesli.

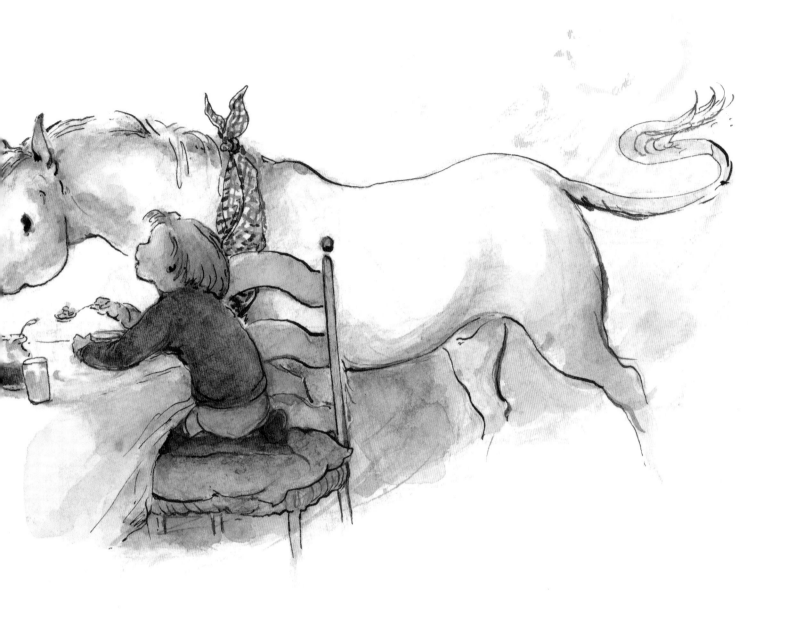

Grandpa coughed gently. 'Maybe a napkin?' he suggested.
Milly tied one around Florian's neck and brushed away the
crumbs. 'Can we put up our decorations today?' she asked.
'Of course,' said Grandpa.

They unpacked Christmas balls, and paper chains,
and fairy lights, and Florian stamped on all the boxes
to make sure nothing could get back in.

Then everyone
helped to decorate the
Christmas tree. Florian
sniffed at the branches
and couldn't help
nibbling them a bit.

'Oh!' said Milly, 'Florian has chewed the star!'
'That won't do at all,' said Grandpa, 'I think we should
go to the Christmas market to buy a new one.'

Florian went too.

Milly and Florian both loved the market.

There were stalls selling gingerbread and biscuits,

toys and candles, and even little wooden Santa Clauses.

Together, Grandpa and Milly chose some decorations for
their tree, and a Christmas garland for Florian.
He was so proud that he trotted around to show it off.
Then he caught sight of something twinkling . . .
something more beautiful even than his garland.

Milly and Grandpa didn't
notice Florian was missing
until they stopped for a
mug of cocoa.

'I thought he was behind us,'
wailed Milly.
'Don't worry,' said Grandpa,
'I'm sure we'll find him!'
But they called and called,
and there was no answer.

Milly ran down the alleys, and looked between
the stalls, and Grandpa puffed along after her.

'Florian! Florian!' yelled Milly,
and she ran into the middle
of the market square.

In front of her was the biggest
Christmas tree she had ever seen.
It was covered in sparkling,
coloured lights. And, at the
foot of it, munching the soft
sweet hay, was Florian!

'Oh Florian! I thought you'd gone!'
cried Milly, hugging him tight.

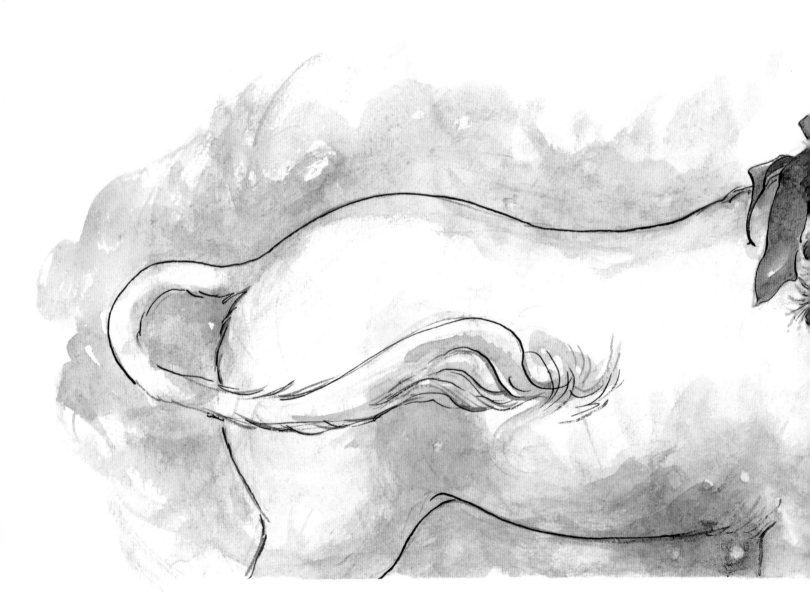

A little girl in plaits came over.
'He's lovely!' she said. 'Is he yours?'
'Yes,' said Milly, 'he's my Christmas unicorn.
Would you like to stroke his nose?'

'Sophie,' called the little girl's mother,
'it's getting late, we should go home.'
'Where do you live?' asked Milly.
'23, Forest Road,' said Sophie.
'Forest Road!' panted Grandpa, who had
just caught up. 'Why, that's where I live.'

So they all walked
home together.

When they reached Grandpa's house
Sophie asked, 'Would you like to come
tobogganing tomorrow?'
'Oh yes please!'
said Milly.

Florian looked over the wide snowy fields to the forest.
He thought of his friends, the fox and the owl.

'It's time for me to go home,' he said.
Milly kissed him and stroked his neck.
'Promise you'll come back,' she said.
'I promise,' said Florian.

Grandpa and Milly watched him gallop away.
Then Grandpa took Milly's hand.
'Let's go inside,' he said.

The front door opened.
'DAD!' yelled Milly.
'I came as soon as I could!' said Dad.

'I've got a new friend to play with in the snow!'
said Milly excitedly. 'She's called Sophie, and
Florian found her!'
Dad looked puzzled. 'Who's Florian?' he asked.

'He's my very own unicorn,' said Milly, 'my Christmas unicorn.'
And she hugged Dad as tightly as she could.

All Milly's Christmas wishes had come true.